LINCOLNSHIRE COUNTY COUNCIL
EDUCATION AND CULTURAL SERVICES.
This book should be returned on or before
the last date shown below.

H30

mine 08/12

03. AUG.

19. MAR. 14.

D0708032

FICTION

08. JAN. 14

LINCOLNSHIRE
COUNTY COUNCIL

This Topsy and Tim book belongs to

_____

Published by Ladybird Books Ltd
80 Strand London WC2R ORL
A Penguin Company

1 3 5 7 9 10 8 6 4 2

© Jean and Gareth Adamson MCMXCV

This edition MMIV
The moral rights of the author/illustrator have been asserted
LADYBIRD and the device of a ladybird are trademarks of Ladybird Books Ltd
All rights reserved. No part of this publication may be reproduced, stored in a retrieval system,
or transmitted in any form or by any means, electronic, mechanical, photocopying, recording or otherwise,
without the prior consent of the copyright owner.

Printed in Italy

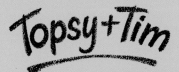

The Big
Surprise

Jean and **Gareth Adamson**

When Topsy and Tim looked out of the window on Thursday morning, they saw Mrs Cowan, the midwife, arriving in her car.

"Hello, Mrs Cowan," shouted Topsy and Tim.
Mrs Cowan waved. "Can't stop now," she called. "I'm in a great hurry!"
And she walked quickly into the bungalow next door, where Mr and Mrs Rupert lived.

Dad helped Topsy and Tim get dressed.
"Where's Mummy?" asked Topsy.
"She'll be back at lunchtime," said Dad.
"We're on our own till then!"

After breakfast, Topsy and Tim helped
Dad with the washing-up.
"I wonder where Mummy is?" said Tim.
"You'll know soon," smiled Dad.
It all seemed very mysterious!

Dad took Topsy and Tim to playgroup.
They were the first children there.
"You *are* bright and early!" said
Miss Maypole.

"Our Mummy has gone away!"
said Tim.
Miss Maypole smiled. "I'm sure she'll
be back soon," she said.

When it was time to go home, Topsy and Tim were the first children at the door. And there was Mummy, waiting to meet them.

"Where have you been, Mummy?" shouted Topsy and Tim together.

"Not very far away," she laughed.

After lunch, Topsy and Tim went out
to play in their own little garden plot.
Topsy found a fat, wriggling worm.
She began to sing a song about it.
"Worm, worm, little fat worm,"
she sang. *"Wriggle and squiggle,
little fat worm."*

Mummy came out to the garden.
"Come with me," she said to
Topsy and Tim. "I have a surprise
to show you."
"Hooray!" shouted Topsy and Tim.
"Ssh," said Mummy. "You'll both
have to be very quiet for this surprise!"

Mummy took Topsy and Tim in to
Mr Rupert's garden next door.
Mr Rupert opened the little gate in the
fence and let them through.
They had never been in Mr Rupert's
garden before. It was very interesting.

Mummy and Mr Rupert led them quietly
down the garden path, till they came to
the big bedroom window at the back of
the house.
"Who's going to look in first?"
Mr Rupert whispered.

"Won't Mrs Rupert be cross if we
look in the window?" asked Tim.
"Not just this once," said
Mr Rupert, softly.
Topsy and Tim climbed up onto a box.

In the bedroom, Mrs Rupert was
bending over a new cot. She lifted a
white bundle from the cot and carried
it close to the window, for Topsy
and Tim to see. A tiny, pink face
was peeping out.
"There!" said Mummy.
"That's baby Robin Rupert,
your new next-door neighbour."

Baby Robin Rupert began to cry –
very loudly!

When Dad came home, Topsy and Tim
told him about their new neighbour.
"He's only *that* big," laughed Topsy,
"but he cries even louder than Tim!"

Match the parents with their babies.

Listen to this rhyme about a baby,
then put the pictures in the right order.

Hush-a-bye, baby, on the tree top,
When the wind blows the cradle will rock.
When the bough breaks, the cradle will fall,
And down will come baby, cradle and all.

Who is older? Who is younger?
Put the children in order, from youngest
to oldest.

Which of these are for a baby?
Which might be for you?